SKATEBOARDING

Jim Fitzpatrick

Rourke
Educational Media

rourkeeducationalmedia.com

Scan for Related Titles
and Teacher Resources

Before Reading:

Building Academic Vocabulary and Background Knowledge

Before reading a book, it is important to tap into what your child or students already know about the topic. This will help them develop their vocabulary, increase their reading comprehension, and make connections across the curriculum.

1. *Look at the cover of the book. What will this book be about?*
2. *What do you already know about the topic?*
3. *Let's study the Table of Contents. What will you learn about in the book's chapters?*
4. *What would you like to learn about this topic? Do you think you might learn about it from this book? Why or why not?*
5. *Use a reading journal to write about your knowledge of this topic. Record what you already know about the topic and what you hope to learn about the topic.*
6. *Read the book.*
7. *In your reading journal, record what you learned about the topic and your response to the book.*
8. *After reading the book complete the activities below.*

Content Area Vocabulary
Read the list. What do these words mean?

brigade
deck
endorsed
kick turn
Ollie
pivot
plywood
roll-in
run
switch stance
tic-tac turn
trucks
urethane

After Reading:

Comprehension and Extension Activity

After reading the book, work on the following questions with your child or students in order to check their level of reading comprehension and content mastery.

1. *Who invented the skateboard trick called the Ollie? (Asking questions)*
2. *Name two different styles of skateboarding. What is different about them? (Infer)*
3. *Who was the youngest competitor to ever compete at the X Games? (Summarize)*
4. *Why do skateboarders use different types of skateboards? (Asking questions)*
5. *Name some of the safety equipment skateboarders wear. Why do they wear this equipment? (Text to self connection)*

Extension Activity

Do you have any skateparks where you live? Do some research and see if you do, then have a parent take you there. Observe the different equipment, types of skateboards the riders are using, and the different tricks and jumps they are performing. Record your findings in a notebook and decide if skateboarding is a sport you would enjoy.

TABLE OF CONTENTS

BIG AIR!

Danny Way kept climbing and climbing. He walked up steep stairways and scaled a series of ladders. Finally, at the top of the Beijing Mega Ramp, Danny looked down. He stood on top of the tallest skateboarding ramp ever built. The Great Wall of China stretched for miles to his left and right. Danny thought, *Wow, this is really big. I'm going to go higher and farther than I've ever gone before.*

First he would drop into the 75 foot (22.9 meter) **roll-in**. Then he would fly over a 61 foot (18.6 meter) gap that spanned the Great Wall. He hoped to safely land on a ramp on the far side of the wall. He would be going 50 miles (80.5 kilometers) per hour. He would have to pull the biggest air of his life—if he can hold on. That was Danny's plan, but on the first **run**, he bailed. Did he have the nerve to try this monster jump again?

GETTING STARTED

Most people don't try to jump over the Great Wall of China on a skateboard! Instead, they enjoy skateboarding in other places. They use public skateparks, city streets, empty swimming pools, and a variety of ramps. Every place has a different kind of challenge. That is the way skateboarders like it, because they each have their own style.

Skateboarding began in Southern California more than 50 years ago. Surfing was a popular sport there, but sometimes the waves in the water were too small to surf. The surfers found a way around that problem. They used skateboards to go

The skills used in surfing easily translate to skateboarding.

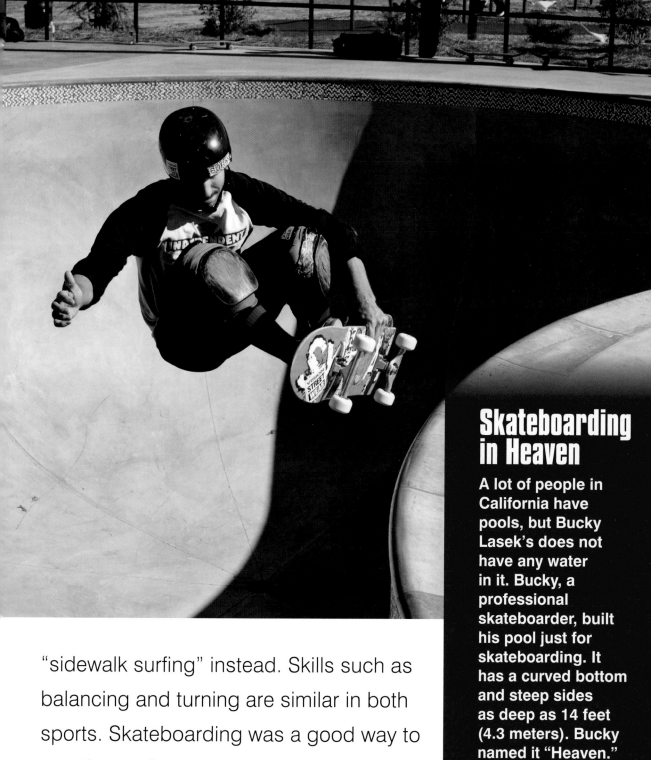

"sidewalk surfing" instead. Skills such as balancing and turning are similar in both sports. Skateboarding was a good way to practice surfing.

Skateboarding in Heaven

A lot of people in California have pools, but Bucky Lasek's does not have any water in it. Bucky, a professional skateboarder, built his pool just for skateboarding. It has a curved bottom and steep sides as deep as 14 feet (4.3 meters). Bucky named it "Heaven."

A little creativity was needed to turn milk crates into scooters.

George "Buster" Wilson grew up in San Diego, California, in the 1920s. He made his own skate scooters by placing wooden fruit crates on top of thin roller skate wheels. When he grew up, Buster taught his sons how to make their own skateboard scooters. This time, he said, "Skip the crates. Just balance on the boards and see where you can go!" Buster's creations became the first skateboards.

The first skateboard sold in a store was produced in the 1950s. The Roller Derby No. 10 Skateboard was very small and had steel wheels. Steel wheels for roller skates were made to use inside, on the wooden floors of roller rinks. Outside, though, they were noisy, dangerous, and difficult to ride. They could not roll over small stones, cracks in the cement, or even a tiny twig. If they hit something, the wheels would just stop rolling. The skateboard and the skateboarder came to a sudden stop.

Early skateboards had thicker boards and metal wheels that did not provide a soft ride.

Urethane wheels soaked up the bumps and made skating faster and more fun.

In the early 1960s, companies that made roller-skate wheels worked to improve them. They wanted to make a wheel that would work both indoors and outdoors. They developed a clay wheel that was a mix of materials. One of these was an early form of plastic. The plastic moved more easily and absorbed bumps. These wheels gave roller skaters more control in rinks. They also helped skateboarders outside. Steel-wheeled skateboards became a thing of the past.

In the early 1970s a new form of plastic called **urethane** was used to make skateboard wheels. Urethane was better than clay. It gave skaters much more control. Urethane wheels rolled well over pavement and wood. Skaters could also go faster on urethane wheels. As they did, they invented new turns and tricks. Skateboards have used urethane wheels ever since. With these improvements, skateboarding was on its way to becoming a competitive sport.

Wide urethane wheels let 1970s skaters do new tricks in empty swimming pools.

Using a ramp to get air is one of the most popular ways skaters try new tricks.

Now more than 15 million people around the world are active skateboarders. As the sport grew, it developed its own culture. In other sports, such as baseball or football, there are umpires and referees. They make sure everybody follows the rules.

Skateboarding is different. It does not come with a rule book. Instead, expectations are based on respect and common sense. The person first in line gets to go first. It is up to each individual to be polite and responsible. Skateboarders learn to get along so that people of all ages and abilities can ride together at a skatepark.

Tommy Guerrero is a respected professional skateboarder. "When I was young I played baseball. I remember the umpire calling me 'out,' but I knew I was safe. What I discovered is that when I was skateboarding no one called me 'out.' It was up to me to make my own decisions, to direct myself," he said.

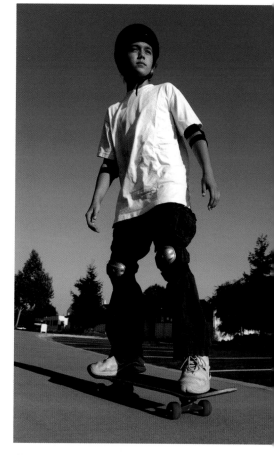

Skateboarding gives many young people a creative way to be active.

SPORTS SKILLS

Learning to balance on the skateboard is the first step for a beginner. Many skaters like to put their left foot forward.

Putting your left foot forward makes you a "regular-foot" skater.

They are called regular-foot skaters. Others prefer having their right foot out front. They are called goofy-foot. Which one are you? Stand on level ground with your feet spread apart and have someone give you a gentle push. Which foot do you step out with to balance yourself? That's probably the foot you would put in front on your skateboard.

Skateboarders balance on one foot and use the other to push themselves

forward. Turning
is the next skill.
In a **kick turn**,
the skateboarder
leans back on
his rear foot and
pushes down
on the tail of
the board. The
front, or nose,
of the board
lifts up. Then
the skateboarder shifts his weight to one
side, and the rear back wheels **pivot** in
that direction, turning the skateboard.
Sometimes skaters turn quickly from right
to left and then back again. This makes the
front wheels clack on the ground with a tic-
tac sound. This is called a **tic-tac turn**.

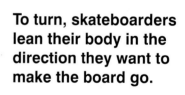

**To turn, skateboarders
lean their body in the
direction they want to
make the board go.**

After skateboarders have mastered kick turns, they can move on to skateboarding's most important trick: the **Ollie**. The Ollie was invented in the 1980s by Alan Gelfand, a young skateboarder in Florida. He liked to skateboard in empty swimming pools. By doing an Ollie, Alan could change direction in mid-air. He'd go up the pool wall, do an Ollie, and then head back down. Alan's Ollie changed skateboarding. It became the stepping-stone to other tricks.

To do an Ollie, skaters first stomp on the board's tail as they lift their forward foot. Then they shift their weight back to the front and push down on the nose of the board to lift up the tail. It all happens very quickly. By doing an Ollie, a skateboarder can actually lift the board off the ground. This lets them jump off ramps or over gaps while keeping the skateboard under their feet as they fly to the other side!

To perform an Ollie: 1. Crouch down with both feet on the board.
2. Stomp down with the back foot while rising up with the other foot.
3. As you jump, the board will rise to meet your feet.

1

2

3

Skateboarders like to develop their own moves and tricks. No two skaters will do things exactly the same way, however, modern skateboarding has a few styles that many skaters use.

Street-style: The first street skaters skated on the street. Today's street-style skateboarding includes skating down stairs, across handrails, curbs, and benches.

Vert: Vert is short for vertical. Going up and down— fast—is the whole idea behind vert skating. Vert skaters zoom up the sides of wooden ramps and empty swimming pools. They use the curves at the bottom to gain momentum to get back to the top.

In vert skating, skaters use a ramp to fly up and do tricks before landing.

Street skating calls for creativity to get over and around obstacles.

Freestyle: Freestyle skateboarders use smooth, flat surfaces as their starting point. They just need a good sidewalk or empty parking lot to do a series of Ollies, kick flips, and other tricks.

TRICK STYLES

In addition to the styles of skateboarding, there are different categories of tricks. Many tricks can be done frontside or backside. Which is which? It depends on the direction the skateboarder is facing and traveling.

Suppose a skater is going to do a trick using a bench beside him. If he is facing the bench, he is doing a frontside trick, because the front of his body is closer to the bench than his back. If he has his back to the bench, it will be a backside trick.

This skater is leaning in to do a frontside move in the direction his toes are pointing.

Imagine two skaters are traveling in the same direction, with the bench in the same place. One is regular-foot and one is goofy-foot. That means they are facing opposite directions. For one skater, the trick will be frontside. For the other skater, it will be backside.

Switch It Up!

Skaters know which foot they like to have forward on the board most of the time. However, sometimes they like to do a trick with the opposite foot forward. This is called riding **switch-stance.**

Skateboarding can be done by yourself or with friends. It takes time and hard work to do it well. Be patient! Beginners sometimes want to rush to learn new tricks. It is better to learn slowly and not skip any steps. Skateboarders spend a lot of hours practicing. They stick with it even when it gets discouraging.

The most important thing is to stay safe as you learn. Skateboards do not have brakes or steering wheels. Many falls happen when skaters go too fast and lose control. Skateboarders may get cuts and scrapes just because they forget their limitations. The worst injuries happen when cars are involved. It's never a good idea to skateboard on a street with vehicles traveling on it. Fortunately, many cities now have public skateparks so skateboarders can practice safely.

Learning to fall safely is part of learning how to skateboard.

Skateparks provide a safe place to skate, far from crowds and cars.

GEAR UP

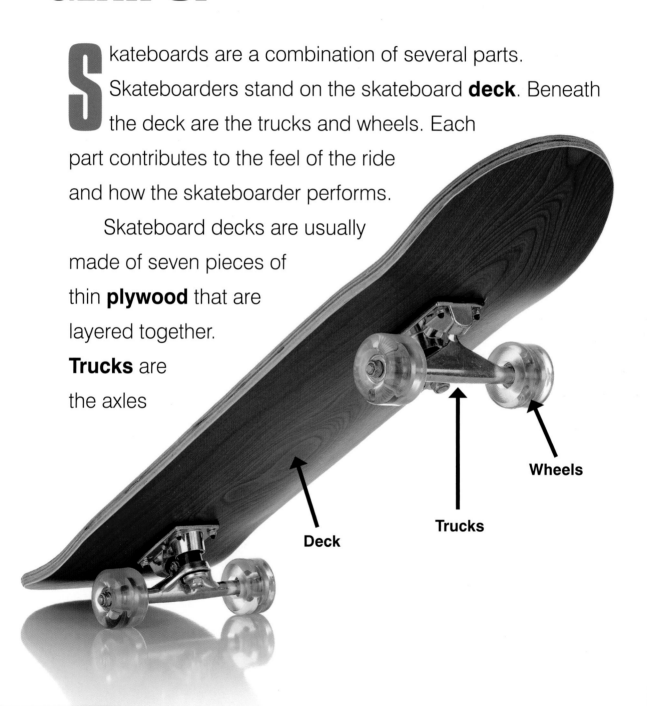

Skateboards are a combination of several parts. Skateboarders stand on the skateboard **deck**. Beneath the deck are the trucks and wheels. Each part contributes to the feel of the ride and how the skateboarder performs.

Skateboard decks are usually made of seven pieces of thin **plywood** that are layered together. **Trucks** are the axles

Wheels

Trucks

Deck

mounted to the bottom of the deck. They hold the wheels in place. The size of each part affects how the skateboard performs. Serious skateboarders look at the overall length and width of the board, the width of the nose and tail, and the distance between the wheels. The type of skating they like to do helps them choose the right skateboard.

Different styles of skateboarding require specific types of boards. Longboards are good for going long distances and making downhill runs. A freestyle skateboarder needs a skateboard that is shorter, narrower, and more lightweight. These are good for the complicated kick and flip turns they do.

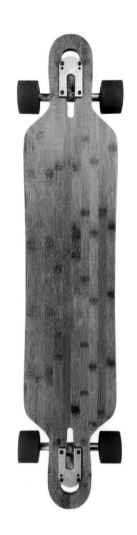

Expert skaters use longboards on steep mountain roads.

A helmet, elbow pads, and knee pads help prevent injuries when skating.

It is important to wear proper safety gear when skateboarding. Head injuries can be dangerous. Professional skateboarders wear helmets when they compete, especially on vert ramps and in pools. They are traveling rapidly along hard concrete surfaces. If they wipe out, it will hurt, but a helmet can protect them from a serious injury.

Sometimes skaters hit their elbows and knees when they fall. They wear cushioned pads to soften the impact and prevent cuts and scrapes. The pads also have a hard plastic surface. When skaters do fall, they practice how to slide out. To do this, they drop to their knees, lean forward on their elbows, and slide to a stop on the smooth plastic.

Looking Good!

Skateboard decks have many designs. They can say a lot about the skater's style and personality. There are designs that are so popular they are displayed in museums. Some people also like to collect original designs from the 1980s.

This skatepark gives skaters lots of options to try new tricks.

Public skateparks give skateboarders a place to practice their skills. They are also a great place to watch other skaters. Every skater has his own style, so this is a good way to learn new tricks.

In the early 1990s there were only three public skateparks in the United States. That has changed a lot. Cities in the US followed the lead of cities in Europe and

Canada, where skateparks were built for young skaters. Now there are more than 2,000 skateparks in the US. More are being built every year. These skateparks often have several sections for different types of skating. For example, some have rails and curbs that street skaters like. Other sections have ramps and pools for vert skating.

The city of Portland, Oregon, has many skateparks. The parks are connected by special "skate-way" streets. Cars and people walking on these streets are warned to look out for skateboarders.

Some skateparks are indoors so people can skate year-round.

Today's skateboarders include professionals who compete in national and international competitions. Some skaters go to the X Games, a competition for intense sports such as skateboarding and snowboarding. Another top event is the Dew Tour, sponsored by Mountain Dew.

Fans pack stadiums to watch the pros take part in the X Games.

The Dew Tour holds contests in cities all over the United States. The Tampa Pro takes place annually in Tampa, Florida. Each year, the organizers design a new course so the skaters always have a challenge.

Winning skaters combine a series of successful tricks into a run. Depending on their style, they might choose a street course, a vert ramp, or an empty pool. Skaters only have 60 to 90 seconds to complete their run and show off their abilities. Judges look at several factors. They like to see skateboarders who are fast and consistent. They also like to see tricks that are original and difficult. The winner is usually the skateboarder who packs in many complex tricks and puts on the best show.

A freestyle skater puts on a series of moves to impress judges.

THE STARS

Millions of people like to skateboard, but only a few can be the very best. Meet some of the sport's stars:

Tony Hawk is one of the best vert skaters of all time.

TONY HAWK

When Tony Hawk started skating at age nine, he had a few things to learn. On his first ride, he rolled to the bottom of the driveway. Then he stopped and shouted back to his brother, "How do I turn?" Tony picked up the sport quickly. He started winning contests and turned pro at age 14. By age 25 Tony had competed in 103 contests and won 73 of them! He was the world champion in vert skating for 12 years in a row. Tony started a company to sell skateboarding clothes and gear, and has a skateboarding video game named after him.

RODNEY MULLEN

Rodney Mullen was one of skateboarding's early stars. He was 10 years old when he started skating in 1977. Within only a few months he was entering—and winning—

Rodney Mullen shows off one of his moves in a photo from the 1980s.

skating competitions. By the 1980s Rodney was inventing his own Ollie and flip tricks that are still used today.

Nyjah Huston is part of a new generation of outstanding skaters.

NYJAH HUSTON

Nyjah Huston was 11 years old when he first competed at the X Games in 2006. He was the youngest one there. He had already been skating more than half his life, though. He started when he was only five. Nyjah has won many skating medals at the X Games and other competitions, and has been in movies about skateboarding. He travels all over the world to perform his amazing street skating tricks.

PAUL RODRIGUEZ, JR.

Paul started skating when he was 12 years old. By age 14 he was famous in the skateboarding world. Paul had a style that made it look easy. "P-Rod," as he is called, joined a team of skateboarders called the City Stars, which allowed him to travel the world. Paul has won four gold medals at the X Games. The sneaker company Nike **endorsed** him as an athlete. He was the first skateboarder to endorse its products.

Paul Rodriguez excels in street skating.

Skateboarding isn't just for boys. Girls have shown that they can pull off gnarly tricks just as well as the guys.

CARA BETH BURNSIDE

Cara Beth Burnside was one of the first female extreme athletes. She worked hard to get there. After she started

Cara Beth Burnside has won gold medals as both a skateboarder in the X Games and as a snowboarder in the Winter Olympics.

skating at age 10, she practiced her tricks for six hours a day! She got so good at skateboarding that she decided to try snowboarding. She has won a lot of medals in both sports.

Leticia Bufoni of Brazil accepts another skating trophy.

LETICIA BUFONI

Leticia Bufoni was born in Brazil, where she started skating at age 10. She was so good at it that she decided to move to California. There, she could enter more competitions and work on her skating career. After she finished her school day at Hollywood High School, Leticia stayed and skated on the school grounds. Now in her twenties, Leticia is one of the best female street skaters in the world.

Skateboarders do not spend all their time getting air. They spend a lot of time on the ground, too. As they develop their skills, they fall a lot. Then they get up and try again. They often spend several hours each day practicing. It can pay off. With dedication and hard work, even young skaters can reach the top of the game.

Fifteen-year-old Tom Schaar is one of those people. When he was six years old, he watched the snowboarder Shaun White try to do a 1080—three full spins in the air. White never succeeded. Still, Tom wanted to try the same thing on his skateboard. It took six years of practice, but in 2012, Tom went to the X Games and landed it. He was the first skateboarder ever to do it.

Alana Smith also made history at the X Games. She liked to watch skateboarding with her dad when she was little. She decided to try it too. She set a goal to compete at the X Games, and got there in 2013, at age 12. She became the youngest competitor ever to win a medal there.

Tom Schaar prepares to conquer a Mega Ramp at the X Games.

You don't have to be a pro to make a great skating video.

VIDEOS

If you can't be out skating, the next best thing is to watch it. There are many movies and videos about skateboarding that show off the talents of the top athletes in the sport. *The Bones **Brigade** Video Show* came out in the 1980s. It was one of the first movies about skateboarding. The Bones Brigade was a group of professional skateboarders. Its members included Tony Hawk, Rodney Mullen, Bucky Lasek, Alan Gelfand, and Mike McGill, among others. Another successful skateboarding movie was called *Ban This*. The skateboard magazine *Thrasher* named it the Best Video of the 1980s.

More skateboarding films came out through the 1990s and 2000s. *Grind* was a popular film that told the story of several skateboarders who wanted to turn professional. Tony Hawk's *Secret Skatepark Tour* videos follow several skaters as they travel the country going to different skateparks. There was also a film about Danny Way's jump over the Great Wall of China called *Waiting for Lightning*. Movies like these make it easy to learn about the stars of skateboarding and see some good action anytime!

The *Bones Brigade* videos helped spread skateboarding culture across the nation.

OVER THE WALL

After building one of the biggest ramps ever, Danny Way had to use it. He was going to try to do a skateboard jump over the enormous Great Wall of China. It took him months to get permission. Then it took weeks to build the ramp and wait for the right moment.

Danny was not new to big jumps. He was one of the best big-air skateboarders in the world. He was named Skateboarder of the Year twice by *Thrasher* magazine. He had a bunch of X Games medals, too. He had soared off his mega ramp time and

Danny Way had to prepare for months for his Great Wall jump.

Danny poses in front of the Great Wall and the Mega Ramp.

time again. But this challenge would be one of the biggest of his life.

He stepped onto the board and started rocketing down the ramp. Suddenly, he realized he had to stop. He was going more than 50 miles (80 kilometers) per hour, but that was not fast enough. He kicked his board away and slid down the mega ramp on his knee pads. He would have to climb back up and try again.

With a hand raised in triumph, Danny soars over the Great Wall!

Danny looked out over the Great Wall and decided to go for it. He started his run and this time he had more than enough speed. He hit the edge of the ramp and flew into the air. His skateboard looked like it was stuck to his feet with glue! Seconds later, he landed on the ramp on the other side. He had done it! Danny jumped the Great Wall!

It was a magical day. Danny did four more jumps and landed every one of them. He got so confident after his second jump he added 360 degree turns on his third run. After his fifth successful jump, China's Minister of Culture presented Danny with a piece of the wall to take home. Lots of people have won skateboard trophies, but only Danny can say he earned that one!

Danny completes one of the most amazing and famous jumps ever.

GLOSSARY

brigade (brih-GADE): a group of people joined together for a single purpose

deck (DEK): the top of a skateboard

endorsed (en-DORSD): offered support or approval for someone

kick turn (KIK turn): a turn in which the skater places his weight to the back of the board, lifts the front wheels, and rotates the rear wheels

Ollie (AH-lee): a trick in which the skater pushes the back of the board to the ground while lifting the front of the board at the same time

pivot (PIV-uht): to rotate something in place

plywood (PLY-wood): a type of wood in which several layers are glued together to make it strong

roll-in (ROLL-in): a move from a flat surface to a curved one, such as a ramp

run (RUN): a series of tricks

switch-stance (SWITCH-stance): a riding position in which the forward foot is the opposite of the one usually used

tic-tac turn (TIK-tak turn): a quick series of kick turns

trucks (TRUX): the axles on the bottom of the skateboard that hold the wheels

urethane (YOOR-uh-thane): a type of strong plastic

INDEX

SHOW WHAT YOU KNOW

1. What other action sport inspired skateboarding?

2. Who invented the Ollie?

3. What are skateboard wheels made from?

4. Who was the top vert skater 12 years in a row?

5. What landmark did Danny Way do a skateboard jump over?

WEBSITES TO VISIT

skateboarding.transworld.net

www.thrashermagazine.com

www.kidzworld.com/article/6543-great-moments-in-skateboarding-history

ABOUT THE AUTHOR

Jim Fitzpatrick has been an active skateboarder since the steel-wheeled days of the 1950s. He was the editor of *Skateboarding Business* and worked for Powell Peralta Skateboards. In 1994 he founded the nonprofit International Association of Skateboard Companies, and is currently vice-president of USA Skateboarding. He lives in Santa Barbara, California, where he and his wife founded Santa Barbara Montessori School in 1975. As a teacher for more than 40 years, Jim is currently the school's principal and still skateboards nearly every day.

Meet The Author!
www.meetREMauthors.com

www.rourkeeducationalmedia.com

PHOTO CREDITS: Cover © TKTKTKT; Interior: AP/Wide World: Jae Hong 36; Roman Vondrous 37. Dreamstime.com: Tomas Del Amo 6; GoldenAngel 13, 26, title page; Russ Ensley 7; Garran3339; Carotip 10; Barsik 12; Sonya Etchison 14; Uptail 16 (3); Homeydesign 18; Charles Knox 21; Denisnata 22; Willie Cole 23; Dmitryzimin 25; Hse0193 28; Steven Jones 29; CarlosPhotos 31; Carlos Calvaho 32; Tom Ferris 34, 35; Rick Becker-lecrkone 40; Carrie Nelson 42. Dollar Photo: alphasport 15; Galina Barskaya 19; Lucky Dragon 20; afxhome 24. Newscom: Tony Donaldson/ICON 30. Pixshark: 33. Red Bull Content Pool: 39; Mike Blaback 43; Hu Jinxi/ImagineChina 44, 45. Courtesy Powell Peralta: 11, 41. Colin Fitzpatrick: 48

Edited by: Keli Sipperley
Produced by Shoreline Publishing Group
Design by: Bill Madrid, Madrid Design

Library of Congress PCN Data

Also Available as:
ROURKE'S
e-Books

Skateboarding / Jim Fitzpatrick
(Intense Sports)
ISBN 978-1-63430-440-5 (hard cover)
ISBN 978-1-63430-540-2 (soft cover)
ISBN 978-1-63430-628-7 (e-Book)
Library of Congress Control Number: 2015932638